Clap

Written by **UNCLE IAN AURORA**

Illustrated by **Natalia MOORE**

Designed by Flowerpot Press
in Franklin, TN.
www.FlowerpotPress.com
Designer: Stephanie Meyers
Editor: Katrine Crow
ROR-0811-0124
ISBN: 978-1-4867-1278-6
Made in China/Fabriqué en Chine

PUT YOUR hands TOGETHER...

This is the book
where we all
clap along
because....

SOMETIMES
a book has
a beat
like a song.

Clap

ONCE

and
WE'RE
STARTED.

Now Clap

Now clap while you stomp down

THREE

TIMES ON THE FLOOR.

Clap **FOUR** Times for me.

Now **Five** Times for you.

Now **Six** Times Together because that's what friends do.

Clap

seven.

now

eight.

Now NINE

and NOW

TEN

Now pause.
Take a
breather.

Now Start

Clapping again!

Clap Really quiet

Now clap Really loud!

Now clap like you're happy.

Now clap like you're proud.

Clap like
it's funny.
Clap like
it's cute.

clap because

Clapping

is just such a hoot!

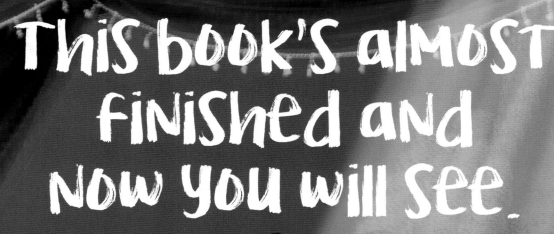

This book's almost finished and now you will see.

So I hope you saved all the strength you'll be needing to clap for my super fantabulous reading!

Now a ROUND of
aPPlause, Please!